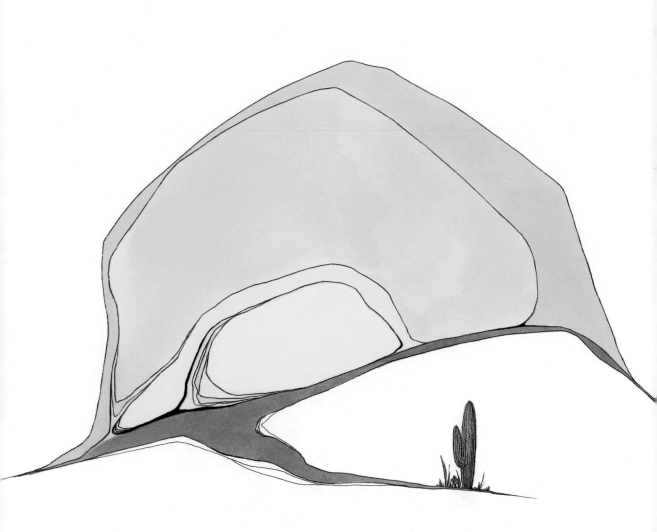

THE DESERT
IS THEIRS

by BYRD BAYLOR
illustrated by PETER PARNALL

ALADDIN PAPERBACKS

Aladdin Paperbacks
An imprint of Simon & Schuster
Children's Publishing Division
1230 Avenue of the Americas
New York, NY 10020
Text copyright © 1975 by Byrd Baylor
Illustrations copyright © 1975 by Peter Parnall

First Aladdin Paperbacks edition, 1975
Printed in Hong Kong

A hardcover edition of *The Desert Is Theirs* is available from
Atheneum Books for Young Readers

19   20

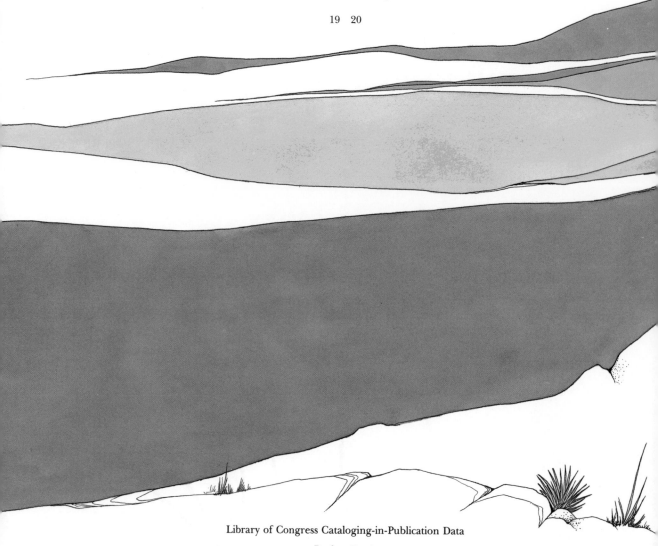

Library of Congress Cataloging-in-Publication Data

Baylor, Byrd.
The desert is theirs.

Summary: Simple text and illustrations describe the characteristics of the desert and its plant,
animal, and human life.
1. Desert ecology—Juvenile literature. 2. Deserts—Juvenile literature. [1. Deserts. 2. Desert ecology.
3. Ecology] I. Parnall, Peter, ill. II. Title. QH541.5.D4B38   1987   508.15′4   86-17323
ISBN 0-689-71105-0 (pbk.)

To Baylor Stanley,
one of the desert people

This is no place
for anyone
who wants
soft hills
and meadows
and everything
green
green
green . . .

This is for hawks
that like only
the loneliest canyons
and lizards
that run
in the hottest sand
and
coyotes
that choose
the rockiest trails.

It's for them.

And for
birds
that nest
in cactus
and sing out over
a thousand thorns
because
they're where
they want to be.

It's for them.

And for
hard skinny plants
that do without water
for months
at a time.

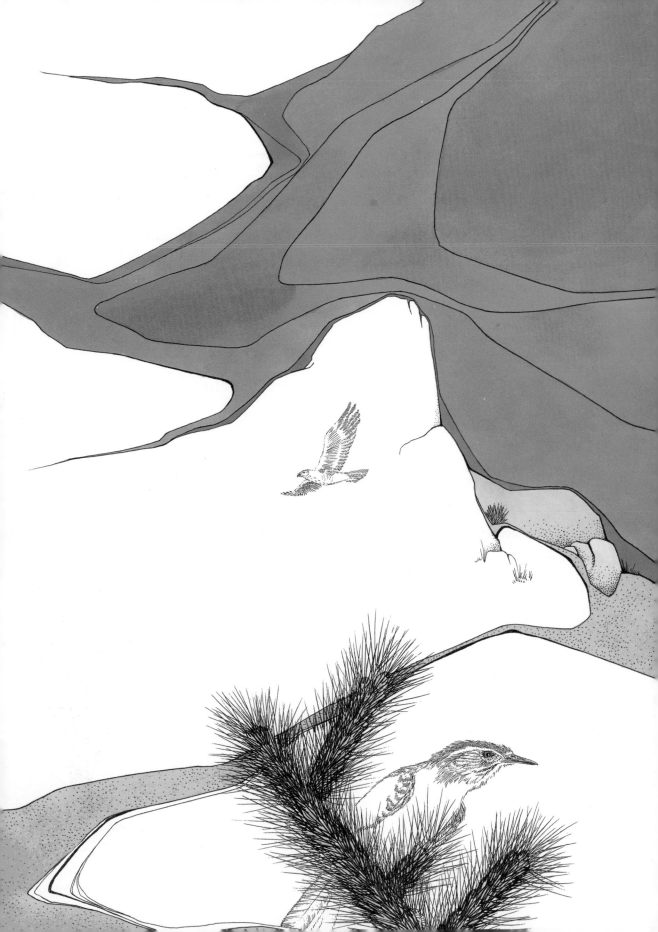

And it's for
strong brown Desert People
who call the earth
their mother.

They *have* to see
mountains
and *have* to see
deserts
every day . . .
or they don't feel right.

They wouldn't leave
even for rivers
or flowers
or bending grass.
They'd miss
the sand too much.
They'd miss
the sun.

So
it's for them.

Talk to Papago Indians.
They're
Desert People.

They know
desert secrets
that no one else
knows.

Ask
how they live
in a place
so harsh and dry.

They'll say
they *like*
the land they live on
so they treat it well —
the way you'd treat
an old friend.
They sing it songs.
They never hurt it.

And the land knows.

Ask why
they chose
a place
where life would be
so hard.

They'll say
that once
at the beginning
of time
Earthmaker
patted out
a dab of dirt
in his hands
and a greasewood bush
grew there.
Greasewood . . .
so you know
it was desert.
You know
it needed
Desert People.

Even then
Coyote
was around
giving advice
and scattering seeds
on the sides
of hills.
Where he dropped
those seeds,
you see
saguaro cactus
growing now.

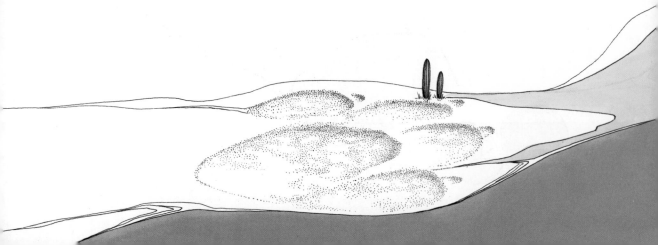

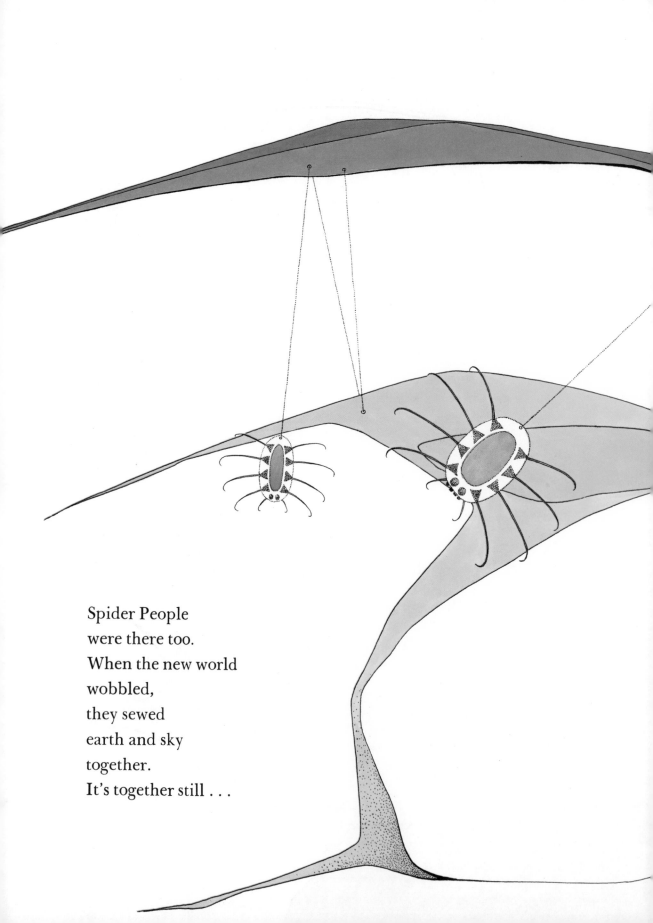

Spider People
were there too.
When the new world
wobbled,
they sewed
earth and sky
together.
It's together still . . .

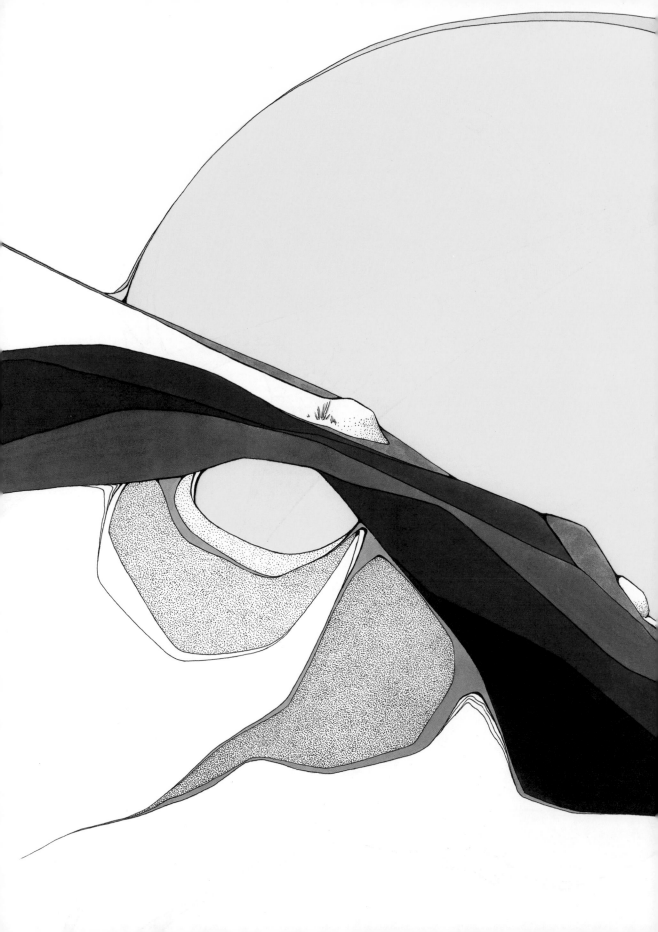

Buzzard made mountains
with his wings

and Gopher
burrowed a path
to lead people
out of the underworld
and up
up
up
into the
fierce white sunlight.

Elder Brother
taught the people
how to live
under the sun.
He gave them
the ceremonies
they would need
for bringing rain.

He even taught them
what songs to sing
to touch
the power
of the earth,
their mother.

And he taught them
to share the land
with animals and birds.

Remember,
animals
were here
first
so they know
better than people
how to live.
Their wisdom
is older.
They're more
at ease
in a desert place,
the Indians say.

You can tell
it's true.

Look how
Badger
burrows
into the
cool dark earth—
while man
has to walk
in the
heat of the sun.

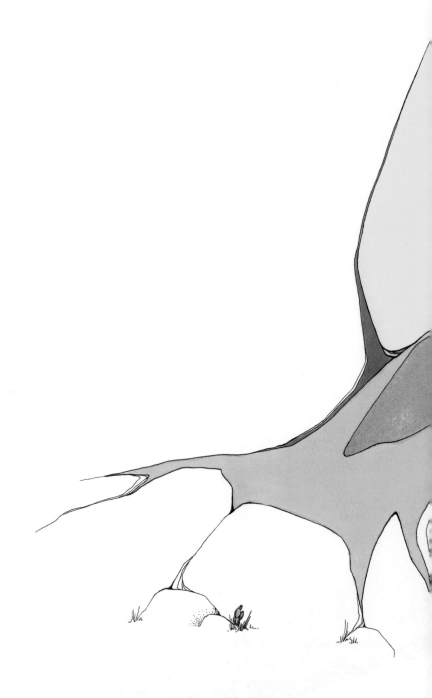

Look how
Hawk
floats
on the wind—
while man
plods slowly
over the rocks.

Papagos try
not to anger
their animal brothers.
They don't
step on
a snake's track
in the sand.
They don't disturb
a fox's bones.
They don't shove
a horned toad
out of the path.
They know
the land belongs
to spider and ant
the same as it does
to people.

They never say,
"This is my land
to do with as I please."
They say,
"We share . . .
we only share."

And they *do* share.

A deer likes
the same sweet seeds
and wild berries
that Indian children hunt.

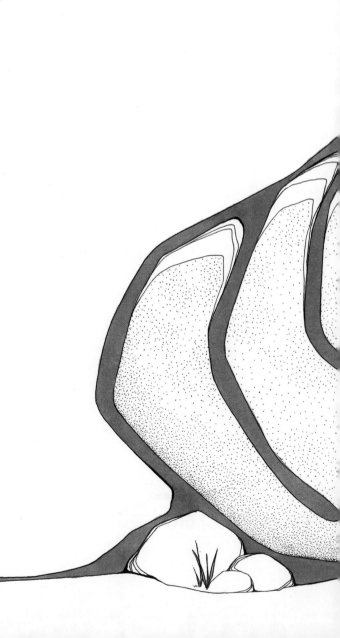

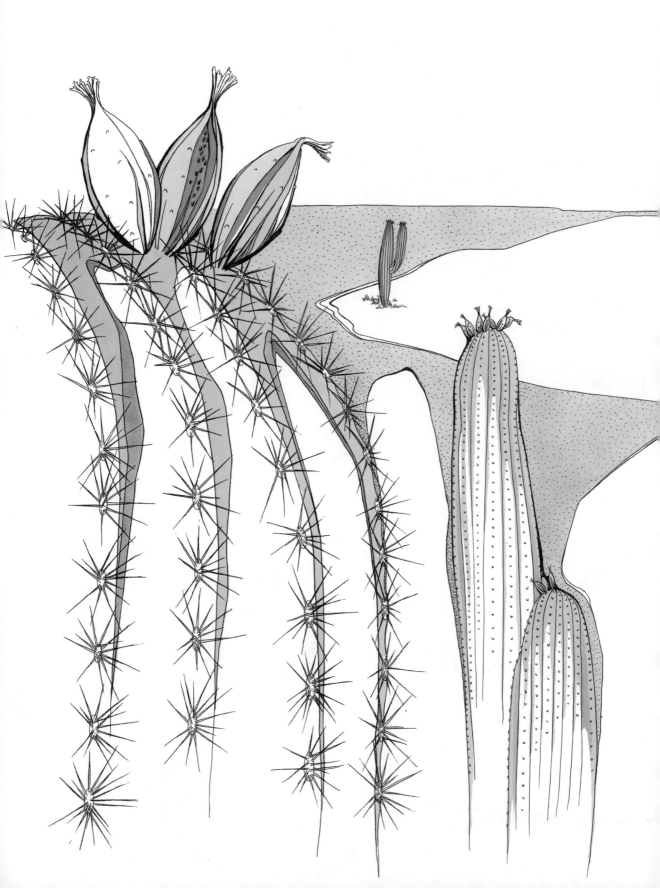

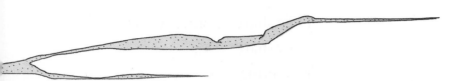

You'll see doves
dipping down
for the
juicy red fruit
that grows high
on a cactus . . .
and you'll see
Indian children
hold out their hands
for the same summer treat.

You'll see pack rats
hiding their treasure,
their good mesquite beans.
But they can't have them all.
People are storing them too.
Pack rats and people both know
to save some for tomorrow—
or later.

The desert gives
what it can
to each of its children.

Women weave grass
into their baskets
and birds weave it
into their nests.

Men dig
in the earth
for soil
to make houses—
little square adobe houses
the color of the hills.
And lizards
dig burrows
in the same
safe earth.

Here animals and people know
what plants to eat
when they are sick.
They know what roots
and weeds
can make them well again.

No one has to tell
Coyote or Deer
and no one has to tell
the Papagos.

They share in other ways too.
They share
the feeling
of being
brothers
in the desert,
of being
desert creatures
together.

A year that is hard
for people
is hard for
scorpions too.
It's hard for everything.

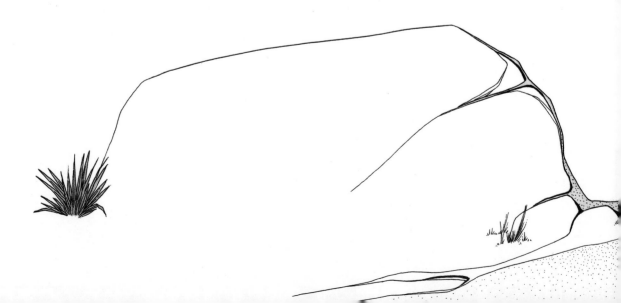

Rain is a blessing
counted
drop
by
drop.
Each plant
finds its own way
to hold
that sudden water.
They don't waste it
on floppy green leaves.
They have thorns
and stickers
and points
instead.

Yucca
sends roots
searching
far far underground—
farther than you'd ever dream
a root
would go.

And Saguaro is fat
after rain—
fat with the water
it's saving
inside its great stem.
Give it one summer storm.
It can last a year
if it has to.
Sometimes it has to.

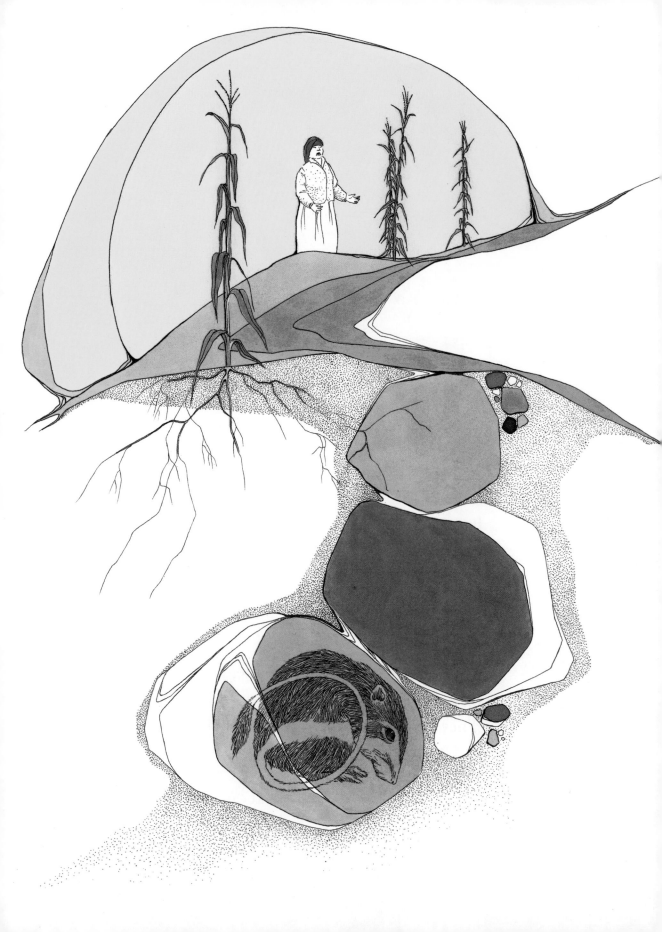

The desert's children
learn to be patient.

Hidden in his burrow,
Kangaroo Rat
spends each long day
waiting
for the heat to fade,
waiting
for darkness
to cool the desert
where he runs.
Just so he runs sometime . . .

A weed
may wait
three years
to bloom.
Just so it blooms sometime . . .

A toad
may wait
for months
to leave
his sandy hiding place
and sing toad songs
after a rain.
Just so he sings sometime . . .

Desert People
are patient too.
You don't see them rushing.
You don't hear them shouting.

They say you plant happier corn
if you take your time
and that squash tastes best
if you've sung it
slow songs
while it's growing.
They do.

Anyway,
the desert has
its own kind of time
 (that doesn't need clocks).
That's
the kind of time
snakes go by
and rains go by
and rocks go by
and Desert People
go by too.

That's why
every desert thing
knows
when the time comes
to celebrate.

Suddenly . . .
All together.
It happens.

Cactus blooms
yellow and pink and purple.
The Papagos begin
their ceremonies
to pull down
rain.
Every plant joins in.
Even the dry earth
makes a sound of joy
when the rain touches.
Hawks call across the canyons.
Children laugh for nothing.
Coyotes dance in the moonlight.

Where else
would
Desert People
want to be?